A Whisper of Southern Lights

ALSO BY TIM LEBBON
(selected bibliography)

THE ASSASSIN SERIES
"Dead Man's Hand"
Pieces of Hate

The Hunt
The Silence
Shadow Men (with Christopher Golden)
The Heretic Land
Coldbrook
Echo City

THE SECRET JOURNEYS OF JACK LONDON
The Wild (with Christopher Golden)
The Sea Wolves (with Christopher Golden)
White Fangs (with Christopher Golden)

TOXIC CITY
London Eye
Reaper's Legacy
Contagion

Star Wars: Dawn of the Jedi—Into the Void
Alien—Out of the Shadows
Predator: Incursion
Alien: Invasion
30 Days of Night: Dear of the Dark
Hellboy: The Fire Wolves

A WHISPER of SOUTHERN LIGHTS

TIM LEBBON

A TOM DOHERTY ASSOCIATES BOOK
NEW YORK

This is a work of fiction. All of the characters, organization, and events portrayed in this novella are either products of the author's imagination or are used fictitiously.

A WHISPER OF SOUTHERN LIGHTS

Copyright © 2008 by Tim Lebbon

Cover art by Gene Mollica
Cover designed by Christine Foltzer

Edited by Lee Harris

A Tor.com Book
Published by Tom Doherty Associates, LLC
175 Fifth Avenue
New York, NY 10010

www.tor.com

Tor® is a registered trademark of Tom Doherty Associates, LLC.

ISBN 978-0-7653-8450-8 (ebook)
ISBN 978-0-7653-9023-3 (trade paperback)

Originally published by Necessary Evil Press, 2008

First Tor.com Edition: May 2016

Let him who desires peace, prepare for war.

—Vegetius, 4th–5th century A.D.

One

THERE WAS HELL ON EARTH, but Gabriel did not care.

It had been over two decades since his last meeting with the demon Temple. That had ended badly for both of them, and since then, Gabriel had been hiding in a dilapidated timber shack in the mountains of British Columbia. In that solitude, he had tended to his injuries and dwelled on the clashes past and those yet to come. His longevity had ceased to amaze him—the decades, the centuries rolled by—but the memory of his slaughtered family still shocked him numb. So long ago, so far away, and yet their deaths were fresh wounds on his soul. Something made sure of that. Made him remember afresh every day. He had defied time, and as if in revenge, time chose not to heal those dreadful wounds.

But over the past three years, as war rolled from one continent and hemisphere to the next, Gabriel had begun searching again. Europe was on fire, the Far East was in turmoil, and it was a good time for evil.

Gabriel knew that Temple would be out there. Drifting, plotting, killing when the mood took him, offering

his services to those who could present the greatest satis-
faction in return: a most challenging murder.

So, Gabriel had immersed himself in the war, seeking
Temple in every place he visited. He travelled to Europe
on a ship carrying tanks and anti-aircraft guns. They
dodged the U-boats stalking the Atlantic, and upon arri-
val in England, he went directly to France. The BEF had
been harried back to the beaches and port of Dunkirk,
and Gabriel worked his way inland as hundreds of thousands were rescued and ferried back across the English
Channel. He sat in a hayloft in France and watched sixty
British prisoners machine-gunned to death. The shooter
was not Temple. In Belgium, he stalked a small group of
British soldiers as they made contact with a fledgling re-
sistance, but the demon did not join their fight. In Germany, there were a million places Temple could be, but
Gabriel found him nowhere. In Dortmund, he heard
whispers of a demon haunting the mountains of Switzer-
land, and he spent months following a shadow. Sometimes, his wounds started to ache and he thought he was
close, and there was a mixture of fear and elation because
he knew this could be the end. *It can't go on forever,* he
thought. *There must be an end, whether fate demands it or
not.* He also knew that there must be a reason, but he had
ceased trying to discern what it could be. The whispers
dried up, the trail grew cold and he found himself edg-

ing farther eastward. In Russia, the war and cold killed millions, and Gabriel searched mountains of corpses for the man with many faces. He heard tales of an immortal fighting with the Russians at Stalingrad, and he spent weeks wandering that frozen, dying city. He walked its perimeter, dodging bullets and bombs and escaping capture by both sides. He saw corpses being eaten and men and women executed for theft. The place was next door to Hell, but he was fast, and he knew how to hide.

He did not find Temple. And he began to despair.

With hundreds of thousands dying each day in Germany, Russia, Britain, France, Italy, North Africa and the Pacific, where was he supposed to look for an assassin? He could wander the streets of bombed cities or the turned soil of death camps, but the chance of them crossing paths when whole nations were in turmoil was remote.

It was early in 1942, whilst he sat in a bomb-blasted garden on the outskirts of a small village in southern Italy, that the land began talking to Gabriel for the very first time.

He had always known the meetings between himself and Temple were far from coincidence. Something brought them together, something guided them, but it was never seen or heard, felt or touched. It was a trace left behind by the man with a snake in his eye, an echo of the carved tree trunks in that woodland clearing of centuries before. But Gabriel had never known its nature.

With the sun scorching down and a soft breeze stirring the air around him, he heard a voice in the scheme of things. Leaves rustled out of time with the breeze; grasses swayed and shimmied; the trunk of a dead tree groaned.

That voice told him of a battle, and a man who was to die.

And Gabriel knew that he had to reach that man before death took him away.

Two

I WAS USED TO BEING AFRAID. I had been close to death many times over the previous few weeks—had shaken hands with it on several occasions—and it felt like a constant part of my life. I had seen my friends die, I had killed and I knew that it was only a matter of time before I was killed as well. I only hoped that it would be a bullet to the head rather than the gut.

We had fought our way down through Malaya, harried all the way by the Japanese. Bombed, mortared and machine-gunned by enemy aircraft, our numbers had dwindled drastically. Hundreds of men had been killed, many more wounded. Those wounded too severely to be moved were left where they fell. We realised later that it would have been far kinder to these poor blokes to have finished them off—the Japs were fond of using injured soldiers for bayonet practice.

Now we were dug in alongside a road leading to Singapore. It was crawling with people fleeing to the city, thinking that they would find safety there. And for a time, I had believed that they would be safe as well. How could such a powerful place fall? How could a fortress like this—defended by ninety thousand troops—succumb to an attack from out of the jungle and across the river?

But the last twenty-four hours had presented a harsh reality: we were going to lose, and the Japanese would take Singapore. Every bullet we fired now, every grenade we threw, was simply delaying the inevitable.

"Really close now," Roger 'Davey' Jones said. He was lying next to me with the stock of his .303 Bren pressed tight to his shoulder. I'd seen him kill three men with a bayonet back in the jungle. He and I had become good friends. "We'll see them soon."

We listened to the sounds of battle from the north. Small arms fire, grenades and the intermittent thump thump of artillery. We still weren't sure whose artillery it was, ours or theirs. Behind us lay Singapore City, and above it hung a thick black cloud from an oil-dump fire. The sky buzzed with aircraft, and miles away, we could hear the sound of aerial bombardment.

Several open trucks trundled along the road. I recognised the dirty white smocks of British nurses straight away. I'd made friends with one of them on the ship on the way over, and I'd often thought about her during the past few weeks, hoping she was still all right. I raised myself from the trench and watched the trucks rumble closer, praying for a familiar face.

"Must be close if they're evacuating the hospitals," Davey said.

"I heard the Japs are massacring the injured."

"Down, Jack!" Davey grabbed my belt and hauled me back into the trench, and then the aircraft roared in.

We'd been bombed and strafed many times since leaving the jungle, but the fear never lessened. It was the growl of the aircraft's engines, the cannon fire, the whistle of the bombs dropping, the impact of their explosions, the stink of battle, the endless crackle of shells striking metal and mud and flesh, and the knowledge of what we would see when it was over. There was never any hope that the planes would miss; we were sitting ducks, and those poor bastards in the trucks didn't stand a chance in Hell.

It was a single aircraft this time, which was something of a blessing, but the pilot was a daring one. Instead of coming in over the fields, he flew straight along the road, cannons spitting death at a hundred rounds per second.

I pressed my face to the mud and squeezed my eyes shut. I could feel the impact of bullets through the ground, as though each death jarred the soil. I heard shouting, screaming, and then an angry roar that made me look up. Davey was kneeling with the Bren cradled in his arms, mouth open in a shout that was swallowed by the gun's violence. He twisted right as the fighter flew overhead, then fell on his side.

I can't die, he'd told me a few days before. *I know something. I know the future of someone, so I can't die.*

"Davey!" I shouted. I scrambled across to him, glancing up to check what the Japanese fighter was doing. It was climbing and turning sharply, coming in for another run. I reached my mate, and the look on his face when he'd told me he couldn't die was already haunting me.

He rolled over and grinned up at me. "Another magazine!" he said. "I think I dinged the bastard that time." Davey lifted the Bren and snapped out the empty magazine, reloading just as the fighter swooped in and opened fire again.

"Stay low!" I shouted, but I don't think Davey heard me. He glanced over my shoulder at the column of trucks carrying injured soldiers and bloodied nurses. His face fell. Then he stood and shouldered the machine gun, legs splayed, and opened fire.

The road exploded, dust and metal and bodies jerking in a chaotic dance as the heavy-calibre shells made a stew of things. I hit the dirt behind Davey, wishing we had more than one Bren. Other men were sheltering, and glancing back, I could see the look in their eyes as they watched Davey stand his ground against the Zero: a mixture of respect and disbelief.

"Davey!" I shouted.

I can't die, he'd said. *I know something . . .*

Davey was lifted from his feet and thrown back over my head. His boots struck my helmet, and I felt blood spatter down across my back and shoulders. For a second, it looked as though he had taken off in pursuit of the Zero, but then he hit the mud behind me, and the fighter twisted away, heading back across the fields.

"Davey," I said, "you can't die." But he was dead already; I could see that. No way a man could survive those injuries. No way.

I went to him first anyway, because he was my friend and he'd have done the same for me. While other men were climbing from their trenches to help out on the road, I knelt at Davey's side and reached for his dog tags.

His hand closed around my wrist. He shouldn't have been able to talk, not with his head damaged like that, but his tongue lolled in his mouth and his remaining eye was a stark white against the blood. It turned and fixed on me.

"Jungle," he said, "saw him in the jungle. Snake in his eye. I knew; I heard and I knew. Terrible things, Jack. Too bad to remember, so I wrote them all down. Can't let the Japs have it. Can't let them know! Find it. Have to find it. One piece of paper . . . but it could change the world. That's what the jungle told me. The trees, the vines, the sound of rain and the song it sang. Change the world."

"Davey, keep still and try not—"

"I'm dead, Jack. The paper. Buried with Mad Meloy."

"Meloy?"

"Jack . . ." His hand tightened, fingers pressing into my skin, but already the look in his eye had changed. He was gone.

Maybe he was dead when I reached him, I thought. *Maybe I imagined all that?*

"Jack?" someone shouted. I looked up to see Sergeant Snelling standing on the road, blood dripping from both hands.

"He's dead," I said.

Snelling glanced down at the ruined body before me. "'Course he is. There're some up here that aren't, so get off your arse."

I spared one final glace back at my dead friend before climbing up onto the road.

He can't have spoken to me, I thought. *His head is almost gone.*

• • •

The road was a scene of chaos and pain. One of the hospital trucks had caught fire, though everyone in its open back already appeared to be dead. It had tipped nose first into the roadside ditch. Some bodies had fallen into the dust, and those still on the truck were adding fuel to the flames.

Several more vehicles had been hit by the cannon fire. People were fleeing their vehicles now that the attack was over, helping each other to the side of the road, where soldiers were trying to help administer first aid. I saw several dead nurses. None of them looked like the friend I had made on the ship, although a couple were too badly disfigured to really tell.

I helped drag bodies from the rear of one truck and line them up beside the road. If we had time, we'd bury them later, but the priority now was to get the survivors on their way.

"Where are you heading?" I asked one young driver. He had a red cross on a band around his sleeve, and he'd painted another on his back.

"Alexandra Hospital," he said. His voice was low and weary, his eyes older than his years.

"Good. You'll be safe there." I helped him smash the remaining glass from his cab's windshield, then guided him along the road so that he could nudge the burning truck aside with his own. It seemed to growl as it moved, as though angry that it was not allowed to burn in peace.

I'd smelled burning flesh many times before, but I never got used to it. It was someone's history going to smoke and ash: hands they'd used to soothe a child, lips they'd used to kiss. I hated that smell.

Once the road was cleared of bodies and broken vehicles, the surviving trucks went on their way. We waved
good-bye. Some of the nurses even managed a smile for
us, though in their eyes I saw a sort of mad, desperate
pity. They knew that we'd be dead soon.

It was days later, while I was lying in the hell of
Changi Prison, that I heard the fate of Alexandra Hospital. The Japanese arrived there, saw the red cross, stormed
the building and over the space of two days put three
hundred people to the bayonet.

. . .

Mad Meloy. Had Davey really mentioned him as he lay
dying? I was not sure, but over the next few hours, as we
awaited the first thrust of the Japanese army, I had time
to dwell on things.

Meloy had died back in the Malayan jungle. He'd
been killed in a vicious firefight with an invisible Japanese enemy. Everything about that brief, terrible battle
had felt wrong. We'd already been fighting for several
days, but when we were ambushed crossing a small river,
it seemed like the end.

The mortars came in first, eruptions of water and
mud that split our group in two, men dashing to either

bank to take up defensive positions. Logic said that the attack was coming from behind, but we had quickly learnt that there was no logic in the jungle. The Japanese knew that too, and they put it to their advantage. They were vicious, disciplined, highly effective fighters, seemingly unafraid of death and able to slip from one place to another without being seen. So, when the gunfire started coming in on us from both sides of the river, confusion came down like a blinding mist.

Shouts, screams, orders barked and carried away by gunfire, more shouting, the sound of people stomping through heavy undergrowth, the thuds of mortar rounds landing in and around the river, rifles cracking through the foliage, submachine guns adding their more consistent crackle . . .

Mad Meloy was close to me and Davey, a grenade in each hand, forefingers around the pins. "Where?" he said. "Where?"

I risked a look above the rock I was sheltering behind. Uphill in the jungle, a swathe of leaves jumped and danced, as though stirred by a localised breeze.

"Eleven o'clock, twenty yards," I shouted.

Meloy nodded at my rifle and Davey's Bren, we nodded back, and he pulled the pins on his grenades.

Two seconds . . . one . . . Davey and I peeked around the rock and fired at the bit of jungle I'd indicated. Meloy stood between us and lobbed the grenades, one after the other. He stood waiting for the explosions.

"Meloy!" Davey yelled. "Get your stupid fucking arse down here!"

The grenades popped, and within their roar I heard the rattle of shrapnel finding trees and bushes.

Meloy dropped beside us and grinned. "Right on their heads," he said.

The fight continued for an hour, and I became separated from Davey and Meloy, holding a position with Sergeant Snelling and several others.

Around midafternoon, the Japanese surprised us and melted away into the jungle, leaving their dead behind. We would encounter these same troops several more times during our retreat to Singapore. They ambushed, engaged us in an hour or two of intense combat, then slipped away to prepare for the next fight.

Thirty percent of our men were dead or injured.

Later, when Davey came out of the jungle, I thought he'd been shot. His eyes were wide and glazed, hands grasping at his chest as though to dig out a bullet. "Meloy's dead," he said.

"No! How?"

"He took three with him. Grenade."

"What else?" Davey was distracted; I could see that. We'd all lost friends and continued to do so, but he and

Meloy had not been especially close. Mad Meloy had not been close to anyone or anything except his own death. *Perhaps all the Japs are like Meloy, and that's why they'll win,* Davey had whispered to me one night.

"Nothing," Davey said.

"Where's Meloy now?"

"I buried him."

"On your own?"

Davey glared at me, his eyes coming to life again. "There was a man. And a snake," he said, then he frowned and looked away. "In his eye." Then he turned and left, offering no more answers.

In the frantic retreat that followed, I had no opportunity to talk to Davey about Meloy's fate and the man with a snake in his eye. And he never mentioned Mad Meloy to me again until that time just before he died.

Or just after.

Three

GABRIEL HID ON THE BANKS of the river overlooking
Singapore Island and the bombed causeway connecting
it to the mainland. He wore no uniform, which meant
that he could be shot as a spy by either side. He carried
no weapons; he had learned long before that it would
take more than a blade or bullet to kill Temple. His eye-
patch was black and studded with three small dia-
monds—a gift from a lady in Verona back in 1922—and
his scar-pocked face resembled the landscape he hid
within. He could smell burning and death, hear the
sounds of battle from the island, and he knew that his
man was over there right now. *Jack Sykes,* the land had
whispered to him in Italy, and he had known instantly
that this was the name of Temple's next intended victim.
It was also a man who posed some sort of danger to Temple. And that was why Gabriel had to find him.

Of course, there was the possibility that he was going
mad.

Three aircraft passed overhead and crossed the strait,
disappearing into the cloud of thick, oily smoke hanging

above the northern part of the city. Gabriel saw the zeros on their wings and knew that they would be unleashing more death within seconds.

His empty eye socket ached, and several miles back, a single, bloody tear had slipped from beneath the eyepatch.

Temple is near, he thought. *Maybe this side of the water, but more likely over there. Looking for Sykes among the soldiers still fighting, or perhaps waiting until they're all taken prisoner. Looking for him to kill him.*

This time, there was no assassination. No money had changed hands; no contract had been set. Temple was doing this for himself, and that, more than anything, meant that Gabriel was closer to defeating him than ever before.

But he had to be careful. The demon might not know for sure that he was there, but he'd be on his guard, as always. Gabriel would be expected.

Blazing oil was slicking across the river and heading around the northern coast of Singapore. There were vague shapes here and there in the flames, and occasionally a smaller blast came from one of these shapes. Small-arms fire sounded all around. Mortar rounds fell, artillery thumped, shells whistled, Zeros streaked overhead and the confusion was aggravated by thick smoke rolling across the landscape.

He heard the screams of the dying and the similar cries of those dealing death.

Gabriel could move between the lines. After centuries seeking and fighting Temple, he had learned the art of invisibility. Not true invisibility—that was something he had never seen, though he had witnessed many strange things—but rather the talent of not being noticed. He could walk through a packed room in a manner that ensured he would not be remembered. If he used public transport, he sat in the middle of the carriage or bus, not at the front or back. He wore old, nondescript clothes, changing his fashions according to time and place. He was never too clean and manicured nor too scruffy. And most of all, he only let the wisdom gathered through centuries of wandering show through when it was most needed. For a man with one eye and the scarred skin of an old shark, this was a talent indeed.

Now the lines were drawing closer together with every explosion and death cry. This battle was heading toward its inevitable conclusion, and while this meant that confusion would reign, it also meant that people would be more on their guard than ever. The fighting men on both sides were tired, exhausted and battle worn. He would have to take care.

• • •

He found a small dinghy washed onto the shore, scarred with bullet holes. It seeped only a little water and still carried its oars, so Gabriel decided to take it across to Singapore. He had considered changing into a dead man's uniform and giving himself up as a prisoner, but that was not the way. For now, he still needed his freedom.

As he shoved the boat back into the water, an incredible weariness pressed down upon him. He groaned and sank beneath its weight, kneeling in the boat's shallow puddles and raising his face to the clouds of battle.

I'm so old, he thought. *Please, let me be.* But he was still unsure to whom he prayed. God was always there for Gabriel, but He was not someone to reason with. Gabriel had not spoken to Him for a long time.

He knelt there for a while, feeling the gravity of his years haul him down. He would be under the ground one day, buried and dead and forgotten, and sometimes, he yearned for that death. But his pursuit of Temple overrode all thoughts of rest. It was not merely vengeance, though the memory of his murdered wife and children always filled Gabriel with brutal rage. It was the task he had been given. The man in the woods had chosen Gabriel for some mystical purpose, and Temple was at the end of every one of Gabriel's thoughts.

Sometimes, he thought they were visions.

He shoved the boat away from shore with one of the oars, sat down and started rowing. The noise around him was devastating, yet for a while, he was contained in his own bubble of calm. The rhythm of the oars, the movement of the boat, the shushing sound of water flowing against the wood, all merged into a soporific spell that lulled Gabriel into peace. He stretched and pulled, and his eyes drooped as the boat made its way toward Singapore.

He said so little but told me so much, he thought, remembering the man with the snake in his eye. *Appeared to me while my family was being killed, disappeared when I returned from finding their bodies. "Feed your hate," he told me. And I've done that. For centuries, I've done that, and every time I meet Temple, it's a feast. I've tasted that demon's blood, and he tastes of human. I've seen his body rent by wounds, but like the carvings in those trees, his wounds seem able to control themselves.*

He rowed, guns spat, bombs fell.

And now something else talks to me. The world is tearing itself apart, and the land tells me a name, and a place, and a reason I have to find this man.

Gabriel had always felt used. In every dark corner he saw the man with the snake in his eye, some perverted grinning monk, a twisted holy man grimacing with mirth while Gabriel suffered not only his own extended life but the memory of the lives of his family cut so short.

His little girl's eyes had been pecked out by a crow.

"Leave me alone," Gabriel said. Something splashed in the water nearby and exploded, sending a mass of water and steam rising high above the dinghy. Gabriel bent forward and covered his head, but the water fell away from him, raising several large waves that almost spilled him into the water.

He continued rowing. It would take some time. And while he took this moment out of the battle, so it roared around him.

• • •

By the time Gabriel reached Singapore, the sounds of fighting were receding. And the pain from the wounds given by Temple down the years was increasing. His eye had bled again, and his chest and ribs were aching as though fires were blazing in his bones.

Gabriel was used to the pain. He shut it out because he knew it would go away. It could not hurt him. It was a memory, not something new, and there were only certain memories that could really hurt.

He tied the boat to a small jetty and climbed out. The

area seemed very quiet, and that put him on edge. From the east and south he heard small-arms fire and artillery, but around here, the battle seemed to have fallen silent. Or perhaps it had simply moved on.

He approached the first of the buildings and peered through a shattered window. A dozen eyes stared back at him, terrified and pleading. "Don't worry," he said, but they were Chinese and did not know his words. He smiled, but that did not work either.

So, he walked on and did not look inside any more buildings. He passed by hundreds of abandoned bicycles and a few bodies, mostly British military. A dog was chewing at one of them, and Gabriel kicked it away. The hound growled and crouched, hackles rising, but Gabriel's stare sent it scampering away.

He looked down at the dead soldier. His hands were tied behind his back, and he'd been stabbed repeatedly in the chest and throat. The next body bore the same signs of savagery, but around the corner he found what he was looking for. The corner of a building had been blasted out by an explosion, and among several dead soldiers lay their weapons.

Gabriel did not like guns. He'd used them many times, but they always led to bad things. He'd shot Temple more than once. It never worked, but there was more than Temple to be cautious about here. There was Hell on Earth, and Gabriel knew that even he could easily disappear into the conflagration of war.

What, then, of Temple? Would the man with the snake in his eye simply find another victim to put on that demon's trail? It was a quandary he had mused over many times before, but one that had no satisfactory answer. The more time passed, the more he believed that this was not simply a feud between two immortal men. It was important. Their fight was a part of history, and its outcome could well change the world.

He picked up a Lee-Enfield rifle, rooted around in a dead man's belt for some spare rounds and carried on.

With every step Gabriel took, the noise of battle seemed to be decreasing. Zeros still winged overhead, but they were no longer bombing and strafing. Artillery sounded in the distance and shells fell a mile or two away, but so irregularly now that Gabriel could distinguish each launch and explosion. He heard the crack of a rifle and then shouting and stamping feet as someone ran. Several voices called out in Japanese, and a machine gun coughed. The running feet stopped.

Gabriel slipped into an open door, glanced around the ransacked hardware shop and sat in the corner. Capitulation. He had known it would come, but not so soon. He'd hoped that he would be able to find Jack Sykes while he was still a fighting man.

He blinked and blood dripped once again from beneath his eye-patch. "Damn you, Temple," he said, and he could imagine the demon's grin, his face flexed and stretched into the image of a victor.

"So, how do I find one man in thousands?" he whispered. The shadows in the shop did not respond, and for that, he was grateful. He smoothed the wood of the rifle and made sure it was loaded. He was still dressed like a spy.

He stayed there for a while, listening to the sounds of war becoming more and more intermittent. People shouted, buildings burned and collapsed, and once he heard a dozen people calling excitedly in Chinese before a hail of gunfire silenced them.

And after the victory, the slaughter. He'd been in many wars and was coming to know the pattern. The victors rarely sat back and enjoyed the end of their campaign, because there was still hatred to vent, and revenge, and the freedom of action that the insanity of war inspired. The thousands dead from the fighting would be joined by thousands more from the surrender, and it would be years or decades before these stories were told.

Gabriel felt distaste at the degradations of humanity, and also at himself for no longer caring. He supposed that, in a way, he was way past human. "You just carry on," he said. "Fight your fight, kill your prisoners. But don't kill mine. Because Jack Sykes knows something I need to hear."

Gabriel stood, shouldered the rifle and walked out into the street. There was one thing he had to find, and then he would be closer to Jack Sykes. He walked for several minutes, searching in bombed trucks and shattered buildings, avoiding a Japanese patrol by standing still in a shadowed doorway. And he eventually found what he wanted on a man lying dead on top of a stone wall. He seemed to have no visible injuries other than a heavy bruise to the temple. Gabriel rolled him behind the wall and undressed. Dead man's clothes.

Four

IN THE END, it was all over even before we reached Singapore. Word came through that we'd surrendered, and an hour later, a cocky little Jap bastard marched down the road, flanked by half a dozen soldiers on both sides. He was carrying a sword. He started shouting, and Sergeant Snelling walked forward warily to meet him. There was an exchange of words, Sarge nodded, and he turned his back on the Jap before saying his final word. I liked that.

"We're to march to Singapore," he said. "Leave all our weapons here. The causeway is fixed and we're to cross it, and on the other side, there'll be transport."

"Transport where, Sarge?" I asked.

"To wherever they want to take us."

"Fuck this!" someone said. The voice was accompanied by the metallic exclamation of a Bren being cocked.

"Don't be so stupid!" Snelling hissed. "You bring down three of them and we'll be slaughtered. You ever think this was going to be an even fight, laddie?"

"You want to give in?" the voice asked.

"Don't talk down to me, you little shit, or once we're

in whatever place they're sending us, I'll come down on you like God with a hangover."

I heard no response, but the offending soldier had obviously seen sense.

Sergeant Snelling walked along the road, telling everyone else the same thing.

We're giving in, I thought. *Davey died for nothing.*

Or maybe not. Maybe the paper buried with Mad Meloy was worth something more than this.

I shook my head. Weird. Battle shock. I smiled as I dropped my gun and put my hands up, and it would be the last time I smiled for a long, long time.

• • •

They made us line up our seriously injured by the roadside. There were fifteen of them, with wounds ranging from bullets in the leg to major head traumas. Some were conscious, some were not.

We thought they were being prepared for transport to a hospital.

Then a hundred Japs emerged from the jungle and walked along the road toward us. They bundled us into three large groups and started us walking, and we all looked back when the first cry came.

They bayoneted all fifteen of them, one after the

other. By the time they reached the last one—a guy from Wales whose name I'd forgotten—he was crying for his mother.

• • •

As I walked, I began to wonder what that piece of paper buried with Mad Meloy might say. Davey reckoned it could change the world. Said he'd seen someone in the jungle with a snake in his eye, and then the jungle had spoken to him and told him truths. Maybe if I really put my mind to it, I could remember where Meloy was buried.

We marched. There were two hundred of us to begin with, generally fit and able-bodied, but the closer we drew to Singapore, the larger our group became. We passed by more injured who had been massacred by the roadside, many of them lying on stretchers and wearing bandages bloodied by their fresh wounds. I could feel anger simmering all along this long road to defeat, but now was not the time.

I glanced around now and then, sizing up the force guarding us. There were too many, and they all carried their rifles and submachine guns at the ready. They had also proved very quickly that they were not afraid of using their bayonets.

Sergeant Snelling came alongside me and we walked silently for a while. When we were on the approach to the waterway separating Singapore from the mainland, the Japanese seemed content to allow us a bit of chatter.

"I never thought it would be this bad," I said.

"Surrendering?" Snelling asked.

I shook my head, nodded at the guards. "Them."

"It won't be like this everywhere," he said. "It's anger. We've killed lots of them, and they're getting their revenge."

"You really think that?" I asked. "They were slaughtering our injured. Where's the revenge in that?"

Snelling looked at me for a long time, his eyes boring into mine as though he could find the answer in me. It made me uncomfortable. I wanted to look away but did not, and when he finally answered, I realised he had been searching deep for some scrap of hope that could explain what was happening to us, and what would happen to us in the future. "Jack," he said, "I just don't know."

We walked into the city.

• • •

Singapore was devastated. Bodies of all nationalities lay everywhere, soldiers and civilians alike, bloated and stinking and buzzing with flies. Hundreds of bicycles lay scattered across the road, and here and there, the owners were tangled with them, metal and flesh fused by heat. Many of the city's surviving inhabitants lined the streets and jeered. I didn't understand.

The closer we came to Changi Prison, the more frequently the guards picked a few prisoners and took them to one side. At first I thought they were singling out people to kill, but when I was jabbed in the shoulder and pulled out of line, I learned the truth. They snatched my watch, made me pull off my wedding ring and took my last pack of cigarettes. Then they shoved me back into the endless flow of prisoners with the point of a bayonet.

I tried to find Sergeant Snelling or my other mates, but it was hopeless.

As we rounded a corner, I saw something that made me pause. Thirty steps ahead marched a tall, broad-shouldered Brit. His hair was sparse and blond, his face burnt by the sun. He was wearing a Japanese uniform at least three sizes too small. He was looking around, stepping this way and that, chatting to a soldier, then moving on to another. He was almost dancing.

Looking for someone, I thought. *I wonder why he hasn't been shot? Perhaps I know who he's after.*

He shifted left, pausing next to a man I instantly recognised as Sergeant Major Snelling. He asked his questions, Snelling shook his head, and the man moved on.

As Changi Jail appeared in the distance, the man changed. It happened in the blink of an eye, and I blinked again to confuse myself more. He was no longer a tall, balding Brit but a shorter, squat Japanese soldier. His uniform now fit him perfectly.

He left the column of prisoners and strode confidently away between a gaggle of Japanese guards.

"What the fuck—"

"What was that?"

"Did you see—"

The commotion spread like ripples in a pond and then calmed just as quickly as guards stepped in, threatening us with their bayonets. But the uncertainty was still there, and the nervousness.

I could not speak.

He'd changed.

As we saw the concrete tower of Changi Prison and a mast bearing the Japanese flag, I managed to sidle up beside Snelling.

"Sergeant Major," I said.

He looked at me, frowning.

"Did you see that bloke?"

Snelling only nodded, looking away.

"What was he after? What did he want? Was he a Jap stooge?"

"Don't think he was, no," Snelling said. He stared up at the Japanese flag as if unwilling to look me in the eye.

"So, what was he after, Sergeant Major?"

"He was asking everyone whether they knew you."

"Me?" I walked on in silence. The shadow of the jail hit us, and I had a terrible premonition that this would be a place of doom and suffering and eternal damnation. I almost turned to run, and as panic rose and clasped my heart, a big hand closed around my bicep.

"Don't worry, Jack," Sergeant Major Snelling said. "I told him no."

Five

THEY TOOK GABRIEL CLOSE to a park at the northern perimeter of Singapore.

"Drop the rifle!" one of them shouted. "Drop the rifle, drop the rifle!"

Gabriel obeyed, and another soldier darted in and snatched it up.

"This way now!" the Japanese said. He was taller than the others, leaner, and there was a splash of blood on his cheek.

"Where are you taking me?" Gabriel asked.

"You're a prisoner now."

Good, Gabriel thought. *One step closer.*

"Your eye?"

Gabriel frowned, then felt the blood dribbling down his face. "An old wound," he said.

The soldier stepped forward and came very close to Gabriel, staring at the patch. "Take it off, throw it here," he said.

Gabriel sighed. He'd liked that lady in Verona. He took off the patch and lobbed it at the soldier, who caught it from the air and plunged it deep into his pocket. He looked up at Gabriel and paused, staring at his hollowed, scarred eye socket.

"Old wound?"

"Very."

"Still bleeding."

"It's been upset."

The soldier stared at Gabriel for a while, his expression perplexed. Then he nodded. "This way."

The four of them moved off alongside the park. They were heading south, deeper into the city, and Gabriel hoped he had done the right thing. He could escape if he wanted to; he was sure of that. But he had no wish to add several bullet and bayonet wounds to his collection of scars.

As they passed the southern tip of the park, Gabriel saw a pile of bodies wearing British uniforms. There must have been at least thirty of them there, gathered around a destroyed machine-gun emplacement. They had obviously been executed—there were no weapons in sight, and some of them were wearing no boots or trousers.

The tall soldier glanced back at Gabriel, then forward again. "Don't worry," he said, obviously confident that his two companions could not understand what he was saying. "Not all Japanese will do that."

"Whose blood is that on your cheek?"

"My own."

As the hours went by, they gathered more prisoners, more guards, and moved farther south.

. . .

They arrived at Changi Prison. Gabriel entered with two dozen others, and he took a while to realise that the Japanese were leaving the POWs on their own. There were guards on the walls and no doubt more stationed outside, but within the main building itself, there were only the defeated.

There were thousands of men inside. There were no toilets that flushed, and the stink was horrendous. Many men still carried food, and they shared it as best they could. Gabriel was just one of many who seemed to be wandering the buildings, searching for their units or friends. Nobody stopped him, though his bloodied eye socket and gnarled face drew curious glances. Eventually, he fashioned a tie from his shirtsleeve, wrapping it around his head and covering the hollowed eye. He hoped that looking like a seasoned soldier would give him anonymity.

Every face he looked at could have been the man he sought. He had no way of finding out without asking, and asking would quickly draw attention. He did not want that.

Because Temple was close.

Even on his approach to the prison, Gabriel had felt fresh stabs of pain emanating from his old wounds. The hatred rose from deep within, familiar as his own heartbeat. But there was also caution and calm, born of his previous encounters with Temple. Neither of them had ever really won, but he knew one day, that would change. One day, he or Temple would be dead, and the world could be a very different place.

Hatred and calmness. Anger and caution. They were strange mixes, and confusing. But one thing Gabriel knew he could trust for sure was the feeling in his wounds.

He entered a small cell—designed for two people but holding eight—and slumped in a corner, shoulder-to-shoulder with a man with a burnt face. He closed his good eye and rested his head back against the wall. He had to think and plan. There was a man to find and a demon to fight once more.

• • •

He dreamed about the Italian garden. There were bullet holes in the building and the garden's boundary wall, leaves and bark blasted from the tree, and the place spoke to him like no other. The dead fruits on the tree resembled his two dead children, and the tree itself was his wife, tall and willowy. In death, she stretched out her arms out to protect her offspring, twisting around them and holding them away from harm. But good intentions cannot divert fate, or a blade, or a bullet or bomb. The fruits were large, ripe and rotten, ruptured by shrapnel and open to the elements. A crow sat on one branch, its beak wet with rancid flesh, and it seemed to laugh at Gabriel as he looked for a stone to throw at it.

It'll take more than a stone, his wife's voice said, *though the tree had not moved. It'll take a change in things.*

"I don't know where I am," Gabriel said. "Am I in Changi Jail or here? Am I alive, or dead?" There was no answer from the tree or the land. "I've never really known where I am," he went on, sad silence the only reply.

And then leaves rustled against the breeze, grass swayed out of rhythm, grains of sand skittered uphill, and their combined whispers gave voice to something that had known about him forever. It was awe inspiring and terrifying, but more than anything, it gave Gabriel a brief, precious moment of peace.

It felt as though he had been noticed.

• • •

Gabriel awoke to find someone staring at him. Temple! He sat up, cringing against the pain of his empty eye, and the man reached out to touch his face.

"Take it easy," he said. "Here. A drink."

Gabriel closed his eye. Temple could be anyone, but he was not this man. There was too much kindness here for even the demon to impersonate.

"Thank you." He took the proffered bottle and drank deep. The water tasted foul but very good.

"You were with the 18th?"

Gabriel frowned, confused for a moment as the remnants of his dream and the real world collided. Then he felt the itch of his unfamiliar uniform. "No," he said. "My uniform was ruined; I had to borrow these." He drank some more. *This is important,* he thought. *I could use this man's help, but he has to believe me. If I make him suspicious . . .*

"You're wounded." The man was looking at Gabriel's face, and in the poor light, his eyes were wide. He seemed to have already sensed that there was something not quite right.

"The eye is an old one," Gabriel said. "The others . . . scars from past battles."

"Which ones?"

"I was in France with the BEF. Hopped on a destroyer at Dunkirk and it was sunk half a mile out."

The man nodded, still eyeing Gabriel's face.

Gabriel had to take control of the conversation. "Surely you don't think I'm one of them?"

The man grinned. "Well, you don't look like a Jap."

"Bastards."

"Aye, you're right there. They killed my mate in front of me. He'd taken shrapnel in the leg and couldn't walk, so . . ." The man's stare moved over Gabriel's shoulder and far away.

"So, what now?" Gabriel asked.

"I guess we stay here."

"I wonder for how long." Both fell silent because neither knew the answer. Others in the cell were chatting quietly, though no one took control to address everyone. Gabriel wondered whether they all knew each other. He'd seen hundreds of prisoners being marched to the jail and thousands more inside, and the chance of finding one man in such a place seemed impossible.

He leaned forward and put his hand on the man's shoulder, and then he injected the weight of all his years into his voice. "I'm looking for someone," he said. "It's important."

"You sound so tired," the man said. "But so alive."

"I am tired. I've been out here a long time."

Perhaps then this man sensed the importance of what Gabriel sought. Because he leaned in closer, staring at

Gabriel's missing eye, and lowered his voice so that it was barely louder than a sigh.

"What's his name?"

"Jack Sykes."

The man shook his head, confused. "But I don't know him."

"I know he's here somewhere. But there's someone else looking . . . a man of many faces. I have to find Sykes first. It's important."

"Important," the man said. "Of course it is. Who are you?"

"My name is Gabriel."

"Like the angel."

"Nothing like the angel."

The man nodded, sat back on his haunches and closed his eyes. For a second, Gabriel thought he had drifted into sleep, removing himself from the sudden strangeness of this conversation and into a protective cocoon of sleep. But then his eyes snapped open again, and he smiled. "Perhaps I can find him for you."

"I'd be grateful for your help."

"Henry." The man held out his hand.

"Henry. Thank you." Gabriel shook his hand and smiled.

Henry stood and walked to the cell door. Outside, there were men lying in corridors, spilling out of other rooms, sleeping beneath broken cisterns; a sea of defeated humanity that exuded hunger and pain in unbearable waves. He stepped into the throng. From his stance, Gabriel knew that Henry was glad of something to distance him from the cloudy future.

How cloudy is my future? he thought. *I have brave young Henry seeking the man I came here to find, but if Temple finds and kills him first, I'm back where I began. And he'll kill Henry, too. Another death seeded in my selfish quest.*

Gabriel wiped another bloody tear from his cheek and waited for things to change.

Six

A DAY AFTER ARRIVING at the jail, they sent us out to cremate bodies.

Singapore was full of them. A thousand dead, maybe tens of thousands, and the Japanese wanted someone else to clean up the mess they had made. So, they chose us, of course. The prisoners, the defeated and dishonoured. They gave us matches and paper and told us to break up furniture and fences, pile bodies and burn the evidence of slaughter.

We worked in small groups watched over by a few guards, and though they seemed more laid-back than during the battle, the Japanese were still very much on the alert. One young lad from our group—can't have been more than eighteen—returned to the jail one night with a pocketful of dates. The guards searched us all on the way in, and when they found the smuggled food, they beat him and tied him to a tree outside the jail, leaving him there all night. We took him down the next day and carried him with us, supporting him all day, afraid that if he fell, the guards would finish him with a bayonet.

I tried not to catch their eyes, because I couldn't hide my hatred.

The more time went by, the worse the job became. Each day in the baking heat, the bodies smelled more, and by the end of the first week, the stench of the city was dreadful. Most of the bodies had been cleared from the streets by then, and we started going into bombed houses and destroyed vehicles. Many of the corpses were already torn up by their violent deaths, worked at by dogs, picked at by birds and beetles and rats.

Each time I added another body part to a funeral pyre, I whispered a few words to God.

And all the time I kept a lookout for that strange man, the one who'd changed before my eyes from a tall Brit into a shorter, stockier Japanese. I tried to convince myself many times that I had not really seen that. Perhaps the heat had got to me, or the pressures of the past few weeks had driven me close to delusion. But it was not the memory of his change that convinced me of what I had seen; it was the memory of my fellow prisoners' reactions.

That, and Sergeant Major Snelling's suggestion that this man had been looking for me.

I had no idea who or what he was, or why he would want me. Perhaps I should have died back in the jungle, and he was the angel of death come to claim my soul.

The food in Changi ran out and we started subsisting on scavenged rice and water. Vitamin deficiency kicked in quickly, and many men developed rice balls—raw, seeping flesh around the scrotum and inner thighs—and happy feet, which weren't happy at all. Somehow, I escaped both afflictions. When most of the bodies had been cleared, the Japs set us to work shifting rubble, pushing aside destroyed vehicles and bringing Singapore's ruined transport network back to some sort of order.

We were working in the courtyard of an expensive manor, burning several bodies and trying to fill a bomb crater, when I saw that man again.

• • •

He marched into the garden, claiming possession of the place with his arrogance. "Jack Sykes!" he shouted. He wore the uniform and the face of a Japanese, but his voice bore no real accent. He could have been anyone. "Jack Sykes!"

I glanced around at my mates. None of them looked at me, because they saw the threat in this man's stance. And maybe they sensed something of his wrongness as well.

Sergeant Major Snelling stood a few paces to my left.

"Easy, Jack," he whispered.

The three Japanese guards who accompanied us seemed unsettled and jumpy. They did not know this man. One of them said something, and the man shouted him down. The guard bowed his head and stepped back, rifle still held across his chest.

"Jack Sykes!" the man shouted again. "Message from home!"

Home! He could not mean that. It was a lie, a lure.

"Easy, Jack," Sergeant Major Snelling whispered again, and the man heard him speak.

"You! To me, now." He was speaking less and less like a Japanese man speaking English.

Something happened to his eyes. I couldn't tell what, but they seemed to shift somehow, as though the sun had moved several hours across the sky in one blink. A ripple of uncertainty passed through the other prisoners, and even the three guards seemed more nervous than before.

This is power, I thought. The man had more power than simple rank could imply.

Snelling walked forward without pause. "There's no Jack Sykes here," he said.

"Come to me and we'll see about that," the man said. "What's your name?"

"Sergeant Major Snelling."

"Snelling. Sounds like an insect. Do insects scare you,

Snelling?"

"No."

"Then what does?"

Snelling did not answer. It was such a strange question, yet so loaded.

"We'll see," the man said. He beckoned Snelling forward, snapping a few orders over his shoulder at the three guards.

"This way." He turned his back on Snelling and walked into the shattered back door of the manor. Snelling followed.

Easy, Jack, he had said. How could I be easy now?

The guards urged us back to work, stealing frequent glances at the manor. We started piling loose soil and rubble into the crater, but without any real effort. All of us—prisoners and guards alike—were waiting to see what happened next.

There was a scream. I'd heard many screams during my war: pleas to God, to life, to Mother, to end pain. But none like this. This was the cry of a man who had seen the end and knew that there was worse to follow. It was an outpouring of every bad thing, and a second after it ended, Snelling ran from the manor.

He was not the man he had been when he went inside. Then he had been proud and defiant; now he was broken. He'd pissed himself, and there were scratches down both cheeks where he had gouged his own skin. He darted across the garden, knocking a fellow POW aside, changing direction, breath hitching in his throat as he tried to scream again. He barrelled into one of the guards, sending him backward into the crater we had been sent there to fill, and the impact changed his direction yet again.

He was running directly toward me when the other two guards shot him.

Sergeant Major Snelling fell a dozen steps away, twitching in the dirt as blood pooled beneath him. The expression on his face had not changed. There was no agony, nor fear of impending death; it was still a mask of terror.

I dashed to his side and held his head, but he was already dead.

The fallen guard crawled from the half-filled crater and snatched up his rifle. He was jabbering at the other two, but all three of them fell silent when the strange man emerged from the manor.

He was flexing his fist, as though he had just held something hot. He was smiling. And he looked directly at me.

"Jack Sykes," he said.

Never in my life had I felt so singled out. Across that ruined landscape, over the back of a dead man, his eyes found and held me like a pin holds a butterfly. I was fixed to the ground, unable to move as he started walking toward me. I sensed other men falling back from me, unwilling to interfere in something that was so obviously not their business.

And was this my business? I could not know. The man would not look away long enough for me to think.

As he walked, he changed. The skin of his face flickered and flowed, as though seen suddenly behind a heat haze. His legs seemed to lengthen and his chest grew broader. He was halfway to me, and now he was a tall blond man, the wrong shape and size for the Japanese army clothes stretched across his body.

"What scares you, Sykes?" he asked, holding out his hand as he skirted the edge of the bomb crater.

What scares me? How could he know? I stepped back but tripped over Snelling's outstretched arm. I went down on my rump, staring at this man, this thing, flesh still flowing across his face as he became one man after another, and I knew none of them.

He was a few steps away when he started to open his outstretched hand.

A shot took him in the shoulder and he grunted, going to one knee in the disturbed soil. Another shot, then another, and I realised that the three Japanese guards must have seen his face.

He was struck in the chest and stomach, the arm and ear, and another impact drove him down onto his side.

I stood and backed away, never taking my eyes from this man and his open hand. There was something there, shimmering in the blazing sun. I could not quite make it out. But I feared it.

The guards were closing in on him now, shooting again as he rolled onto his back and reached for a cloud. A bullet smashed his hand aside in a mist of blood, and I turned and ran. My mates were already a hundred yards along the street, ducking behind a wrecked truck to dodge the bullets and perhaps also the sight of that strange man being shot to pieces.

He knows me, I thought. *He knows my name, and maybe if he'd had another second, he'd have shown me . . .* "What scares you, Sykes?" he had asked. Perhaps he knew.

Something whistled past my ear and I heard the shot, then the shouts and the sound of boots hitting dirt as the guards chased us. I stopped in the middle of the street with my arms held high, cringing, expecting a bullet or bayonet between my shoulder blades at any second. But the guards only gathered us together and hustled us away, heading back to Changi. They were quieter than usual, less cruel, and I took advantage of the leisurely pace to gather my thoughts.

None of the other men talked to me. They had heard him calling my name.

• • •

We were searched as thoroughly as ever upon our return to Changi, and then let inside under our own steam. I parted from the others and made my way into the main building, climbing staircases that were now home to dozens of men, finding my cell, grabbing my meager belongings and leaving. I had to find somewhere else to sleep. I craved the company of strangers.

More than anything, I needed to think about what had happened.

"Sykes," a voice said.

I gasped and spun around on the landing. There were men all around me, sitting in hallways, leaning against doors, talking and smoking and sleeping. I tried to see where the voice had come from. I dreaded seeing that shifting face again.

He was shot, I thought. A dozen times or more . . . he was dead.

"Sykes, here." A man stepped from the shadows of a doorway and motioned me toward him.

"You stay away from me," I said. I backed away, keeping my voice low. "Just stay away."

"Sykes, someone needs to see you." He was following me, a short, thin man with a wound to the side of his neck. "He's been looking for you, says it's something important. His name's Gabriel, like the angel."

"How do you know my name?"

"I heard from a lad I know that you ran into a bit of trouble on your work party today. Japs shot someone who attacked you and your sergeant major."

"And how many names do you have?"

The man frowned and shook his head. "My name's Henry."

I saw nothing in his face or eyes to reveal a lie. My heart thudded in my chest, and my vision throbbed with each heartbeat. I was badly scared. I'd seen something that I could not even begin to explain, and there was a hot patch on the back of my neck, as if someone was staring at me.

"What does this Gabriel want?"

Henry shrugged. "I don't know. But I think he's been looking for a while. He's old."

"How old?"

Henry shrugged, frowning again. "I dunno. There's just something about him."

"His face changes," I said. I had to get away. I had to run, flee . . . but I was a prisoner there. A rat in a trap waiting to be killed.

"No," Henry said. "But I'm sure he wishes it could. Follow me if you like. He said it was important. Don't know how or why, but I believe him." Henry turned and walked away along the landing.

I followed. I should have gone in the opposite direction, exploring the depths of the prison until I found somewhere dark to hide. But I was suddenly tired and depressed, driven down by everything I had seen, scared at whatever was to come. Some said the Japanese were going to leave us here to rot, while others heard rumours of work parties being sent up-country to work on roads and railways. The future felt bleak.

We moved through the prison, and the stink and sounds of that place could have been lifted straight from Hell.

Seven

AND THERE HE WAS.

Gabriel knew that the man who walked through the door behind Henry was Jack Sykes. He had never seen him, had no hint from the voice of the land of what he looked like, but he knew that he had his man.

Temple will be on his trail, he thought. But he blinked, and listened to his own pain, and the demon was not close.

"Are you him?" Sykes asked. He was standing in the doorway, tensed and ready to run. Henry had already sat down against a wall, and the others from the cell had gone to search for food.

"No," Gabriel said. "You've seen him?"

Sykes nodded, and Gabriel knew that he was telling the truth.

"You saw him and lived." He could not keep the amazement from his voice.

"The Japs shot him to pieces," Sykes said. "He's dead."

Gabriel shook his head. "Not dead," he said. "Probably crawled off somewhere to recover. Did he show you his hand?"

"He meant to. He had something there, but . . . Who is he?"

"His name is Temple. He's also the Twin, a thing of many faces. And you know something about him that I need."

Sykes walked fully into the cell and squatted by the door. He grimaced as his knees popped. He wiped sweat from his face and rested his elbows on his knees. "I don't know anything about him," he said. "Only that he's wrong."

"You do know something. You have to. Something that gives him reason to seek you out and kill you."

"He wants to kill me?"

"Yes. He's an assassin."

"Who would want to assassinate me?"

"Only Temple. It's a private affair this time."

Sykes rested his head back against the wall and closed his eyes.

"A story," Gabriel said. "A myth. Something you heard but didn't believe, a phrase you could not understand. Somewhere in the jungle, perhaps? Think. It could be the demon's downfall."

"Demon?" Sykes's eyes snapped open.

Gabriel took in a deep breath, and his missing eye pained him. He sighed. "Yes, I used that word," he said.

"Demon." Sykes closed his eyes again. "A demon, trying to kill me. You hear that, Henry?"

"I hear," Henry said.

Gabriel stood and went to Sykes, kneeling beside him and wanting to hold him tight. "Do you believe in demons?" he asked.

Sykes opened his eyes and stared at Gabriel's empty eye socket. His face was expressionless. "You're bleeding," he said after a while, and he pushed himself to his feet.

Gabriel stood and dabbed at his eye. "Jack Sykes, what do you know?"

"I had a friend," Sykes said. "He was killed on the mainland. He raved. He said he saw something in the jungle, a man with a snake in his eye. And he knew things that he wrote down and buried with a dead man."

Snake in his eye! Gabriel gasped, and the pain of his wounds made itself known. *Snake in his eye! That man, that preacher, that monster in the woods on the day my family were slaughtered.* He groaned and leaned against a wall, watching blood drip from his ruined eye as though he were seeing violence from long ago.

"What's wrong?" Sykes asked.

"He's nearer!" Gabriel reached for Sykes, grasping his shirt and pulling him close so that their noses were almost touching. "We have to find that grave," he said.

"Your friend may have seen or heard something that could help me."

"Help you with what?"

Gabriel tried to blink away the pain, but it would not go. He took in a deep, replenishing breath, but all movement hurt. "Help me die in peace."

He nodded his thanks to Henry, dragged Sykes from the cell and tried to decide which way to go.

Eight

WE LEFT CHANGI JAIL. We had only been there for a few days, and the layout of the place was still a mystery to me. But even though Gabriel said he had been there no longer than me, he seemed to know his way around, familiar with where doorways and passages and staircases would be. He led us deep, and in the depths of the jail we found places where men had gone to die. They lay along corridors, in subterranean rooms and on stairs, drinking feebly, moaning, many of them already dead. I could smell their wounds and taste the hopelessness of a hundred last breaths. Some of them seemed to recognise that we had escape on our minds, because they raised themselves up on bony elbows and smiled us on.

Most of them were wounded, but some were diseased. I'd seen it before in the jungle, but here, there were no medicines and no one to help, so the sick resigned themselves to their fate.

"How can the officers just leave these men down here?" I asked.

Gabriel only shrugged. He spoke little, and I'd come

to learn that all of what he said had to do with his quest for the being called Temple.

We went lower, and in a corridor ankle-deep in oily water we found several doors leading into boiler and plant rooms. Two rooms were black with coal dust but now completely empty of coal. Another two rooms contained giant, dead machinery. Water leaked from cracked pipes and dripped from the machines. I found it an eerie, disturbing place.

"We'll go this way," Gabriel said. He pointed to a room at the end of the corridor that had barely been formed out of the rocky ground. There was an open doorway set in the concrete wall, but beyond, when it was illuminated by a heavy lantern Gabriel found in the plant room, I saw only bare rock. It was an unfinished room, entry to a ghost wing of the prison that had never been built.

"So, we dig through rock," I said. "A tunnel. Genius." I'd expected much more from this man. I'd been waiting for him to lead us to a hidden doorway to the outside. A route back to Britain, perhaps, bypassing all that painful, cruel distance in between.

"A ready-made tunnel," he said. "Look." He shone the lantern to the left, and the light slid from the curve of a manmade form.

I went closer to inspect it and found the large, wide

head of a pipe curved up from the ground. "Drain?" I asked.

Gabriel nodded. "Our way out. Now let's break it open."

"What sort of drain?" He did not answer, and as we went to work with rusty tools I began to wonder just what we would discover upon breaking the pipe.

• • •

Days earlier, when we had first arrived, there had been running water. Pipes hammered with fluctuating pressure, toilets flushed, we drank and washed. But soon after, the water supply failed. Toilets rapidly became unusable, and men found other places to defecate.

The drain was tall enough to walk in, and knee-deep in shit.

I fell back when the shell of the pipe broke, forced away by the stink that gushed from the rupture. Gabriel glanced at me and hit the drain again, shattering a large portion of it with one careful blow. He leaned and shone the lantern both ways.

I heard things running, splashing and squealing in there. I gagged, calmed myself, then retched a thin, painful fluid. There was little food for me to bring up, and my puke was a sickly green.

"We have no choice," Gabriel said.

"I do. I'm not crawling through that only to be—"

He shone the lantern at the ceiling so that it illuminated both of our faces equally, then came closer and stood before me. "We have no choice," he said again. He carried no gun or knife, but I heard the threat in his voice.

"So is this kidnapping now?" I asked.

"Rescue."

"Even if I don't want to be rescued?"

"You want to stay? Do you? You know what they're like. You know what's going to happen to most of those men up there; they'll be used as slave labour up-country, then executed when they become unfit."

"That's just a rumour."

"It's a fact. The Japanese have no respect for surrender."

"So if I do decide to stay . . ."

Gabriel leaned in closer, and I could smell something on his breath that I did not like: age. He was an old, old man, even though he appeared only a few years older than me.

"You can't stay," he said. "We have to find the grave your friend dug and read the note he left. It's important."

"For you."

"Perhaps not only for me. I don't know. I'm still no closer to understanding."

I approached the fractured drain, trying to breathe lightly. But nothing could hide that stink.

"How long is this?" I asked.

"I have no idea."

"But you knew it was here?"

"I surmised."

I nodded. "You go first."

. . .

The stuff in the drain had a crust across the top of it. I hoped it would hold our weight, but it crumpled and cracked and our feet went through, and that disgusting mess came up to just above my knees, warm and vile, and there were things running across the hardened surface, rats and beetles and fat spiders whose weight could be easily supported. I caught only brief glimpses of them as Gabriel swung the lantern by his side, and I puked again at the smells that rose around us. There was no air movement at all down there, nothing to purge my lungs, and every minute I grew more amazed that I was still alive. We moved on, crunching and slopping, and the mess seemed to be getting deeper the farther away from the prison we went.

"Will he follow?" I asked.

Gabriel turned around, and I noticed the blood dripping from his eye, the pain etched into every scar and wound on his face. "He already is."

• • •

In the end, we came to a large domed junction, a collection point that drained into a larger tunnel that led to the river. It was too deep to walk. We had to swim.

Nine

FOR THE LAST HOUR, Gabriel had been struggling against the pain. Temple must be so close for it to be this bad, but however hard he listened, he could hear no signs of pursuit. Perhaps the Twin was above ground, following the route of their escape across the prison yard and surrounding area. If so, they would exit the sewer into a storm of violence. And Gabriel felt in no shape for a fight.

At least the stink might distract Temple for a precious few seconds.

After an age, he sensed the first gleam of natural light from ahead. He told Sykes to stop, and saw a definite sheen of silvery light across the fetid water surface. He even sensed a whiff of fresh air below the stench, and he turned to Sykes. The soldier already knew, and he smiled through a mask of muck.

"Almost out," Gabriel said.

"And the demon?"

"Close. We'll wait at the end of the pipe for a while. Then I'll go out, see what's around, and we decide our next step from there."

"I don't understand what this is all about," Sykes said. The look of bewilderment in his eyes spoke volumes.

"We can talk more," Gabriel said. "Away from Singapore, back in the jungles, there'll be time."

Sykes nodded, but he did not seem comforted. He had already been through those jungles, and they had been bad for him. Gabriel could empathise. He had lived through many bad times, and the sense of dread Sykes must be feeling was as familiar as breathing.

They came close to the end of the pipe and revelled in the fresher air wafting in from outside. Gabriel motioned to Sykes to keep still and waded on alone. Each movement stirred up a stink. Things bumped against his legs, and some of them swam away. He tried not to think about the infections he and Sykes might be picking up. *Almost there,* he thought.

The sun was dipping toward the horizon, setting the warm air alight. Gabriel squatted at the end of the pipe for a while, breathing in the fresher air and enjoying the sensation as it moved against his sweaty skin. *Where is he?* he thought. The familiar pains and aches were still there, though they seemed to have lessened again. Perhaps at some point during their nightmare escape, Temple had crossed their path on the ground above. So close.

Gabriel searched the marshy area around the pipe's outflow for signs of movement. A few birds waded here and there, and things slipped into and out of the water, skins slick and camouflaged with effluent. He stood slowly, held onto the rough upper curve of the pipe and looked back toward Changi Jail. The prison wall, tall and blank, caught some of the setting sun. There were a couple of shapes walking the wall—probably Japanese guards—but they would never see him from that distance. Ahead of him, across the boggy ground, a few trees marked the place where he and Sykes should head. From there, more hiding and slinking until they bypassed Changi Village and made it to the water. Steal a boat, make their way to the mainland, then travel back up through Malaya to the site of Jack Sykes's friend's rough grave.

And all the time, Temple would be searching for them. And as usual, he had death on his mind.

Gabriel took one more look around, then ducked back inside to fetch Sykes.

• • •

Seconds after starting across open ground, they heard voices.

"Stop!" Gabriel whispered. He sank to his knees, and Sykes followed suit.

The voices came from ahead of them, before the trees

at the edge of the bog, their owners probably hidden away by a clump of bushes. They were Japanese.

"Slowly, back."

"To the drain?"

"For now."

As they started moving back, a Japanese soldier stood a dozen steps ahead of them, slung his rifle over his shoulder and walked along a low ridge of rock. He was muttering to himself, laughing, sniggering and then muttering again. *Telling himself a joke,* Gabriel thought. *I hope it's funny enough to keep him occupied until—*

The soldier paused and raised his head. He looked directly at Gabriel, and for a few seconds, his expression did not change. Whether it was surprise, shock or the joke still clearing itself from his senses, Gabriel had time to reach into his sock and pull out the throwing knife he had acquired during his first day in Changi.

"Jesus," Sykes said, and his voice galvanised the surprised soldier.

The soldier had time to shout before Gabriel's knife struck him in the throat. He fell back, rifle slipping from his shoulder, and there was a dull splash as he disappeared from sight.

Two other soldiers stood, already training their rifles in Gabriel's and Sykes's direction.

"Get his rifle!" Gabriel shouted, and then he was

moving. He ran straight at the men, growling, hands raised like claws, blood streaking his face from the mutilated eye socket, clothes covered in stinking water and shit, and he was something they had never seen before. One tried to fire, but his safety must have been on. The other was stepping backward, shaking his head as though to clear this gruesome vision. Gabriel reached them, snatched the rifle from the closest soldier's hands, reversed it and slashed him across the face with his own bayonet.

As the first soldier went down, hissing through slashed cheeks and lips, the second found his confidence and raised his rifle.

Gabriel knew that any shooting would draw instant attention, and their escape would be thwarted. Not only that, but Temple would be drawn to the violence. Their showdown would come much sooner than Gabriel had hoped for, and any chance of finding the grave would be long gone.

He threw the rifle like a spear. It had no chance of working, but he hoped it would give him enough time to make it across the muddy ground to the last man standing.

The guard shouted something and knocked the rifle aside with his own. He took aim again, and Gabriel could see that he had gathered his senses.

One second; that was all he had.

He fell to the ground and rolled, passing over the thrashing soldier, whose hands clutched at his slashed face, lifting him as he went to stand again, hoping to use him as a shield.

The second soldier came at Gabriel, rifle still raised and looking for a shot.

Sykes stood. He swung the liberated rifle, and though this one did not have its bayonet attached, the stock made a satisfying thump as it struck the soldier's head. He dropped his rifle and went down, reaching out just in time to prevent himself taking in a mouthful of rancid water. Sykes was on him quickly, swinging the rifle again. Then he stood on the semi-conscious soldier's head and pressed his face down into the mud. He looked away as the final bubbles rose.

Gabriel wrapped his arm around the head of the man with the slashed face and broke his neck.

Sykes came to his side, panting, shaking, sweating. "Do you think they heard?"

Gabriel looked across at the prison. There was no sign of activity, no running men or revving motors. "No," he said. "But they'll soon be missed. We have to move."

The man with Gabriel's knife in his throat was still moving feebly as blood gushed from the wound. One clawed hand reached for the knife but seemed unable to find it.

"Us or them," Gabriel said.

Sykes nodded, moving away.

They slipped between the trees, still crouched low in case anyone was watching from the prison. They moved quickly, eager to put distance between themselves and the jail before nightfall.

Long way to go, Gabriel thought, *but moving away from Temple feels good. Feels as though I'm going in the right direction for the first time in a long while. Heading for something meaningful. Whatever the hell is in that grave better be worth this.*

Night fell, the men ran and time moved them closer to the end.

Ten

I KNEW BY THEN that he was not a man. Gabriel had told me that a demon wanted me dead, but he had yet to talk about himself. About why he wanted me alive, and needed to find Mad Meloy's grave, and why whatever Davey had written down and buried with Meloy might be so important.

I was just a soldier. I had fought my way down through Malaya, been captured when Singapore fell, imprisoned, escaped, and now I was on the run with . . . something that was not a man.

Then what was he?

Escape from Changi Village was easier than I could have expected. Getting out of the jail itself had been difficult, but the area of Changi was left mostly to the prisoners, with Japanese guarding the outer extremes only. We made it to the sea, dodged a couple of patrols and found a boat to steal. Before launching, I told Gabriel I needed food and water. He seemed impatient but nodded and told me not to be long. I left, heading for a house that looked abandoned, wondering whether he even needed to eat or drink at all.

I found some tinned food and a tank of water, warm but sweet. I opened two tins and ate a meal, careful not to give my starved stomach too much of a shock.

It was a small, well-kept home, and I wondered what had become of its occupants. There were no pictures and little to indicate who had lived there. I took a quick look around for weapons and found some knives in the kitchen. They were very sharp, and I slid a couple into my belt.

Gabriel was sitting beside the boat as I approached. "We have to go now," he said.

"I found some food and a couple of knives."

"Good. In the boat."

"Is he coming?"

"He's closer than before."

We launched the boat and climbed in, taking turns at the oars. When Gabriel rowed, he stared over my shoulder, back at the land we had just left. Sometimes, he winced in pain. Once away from the land, we both took a minute to dip in and wash away some of the filth. I felt better, but I thought that even if I bathed forever, the smell of my escape would still be upon me.

Even with the looming threat behind us, I found the sound of the oars dipping into the water soporific.

"So, are you going to tell me anything?" I asked.

Gabriel smiled, and it shocked me. I had not seen it before. It did not suit his face. "You'd never believe me."

"Try."

"I can't. I don't. All the people I've met . . . I've never really explained what I'm doing. I don't know myself."

"Is it revenge?"

"Yes, revenge. Is it that obvious?"

I nodded. "And you're not a soldier."

Gabriel stopped rowing. "Is that obvious, too?"

"It was a guess, but I was pretty sure. So, what are you? Spy? Special Operations?"

"None of that." He seemed almost disappointed, as though he wished I could guess more.

"So, Temple . . . this demon, this Twin thing . . . killed someone you cared for?"

He stared over my shoulder again, but he was seeing something far more distant than the shores of Singapore. He rowed, arms reaching, shoulders flexing, and the whole movement—Gabriel, the boat, the water—was unbelievably calming. "Yes, that's what he did."

"And the man with the snake in his eye?"

He stared at me with his one piercing eye, and I felt naked beneath his scrutiny.

"Sorry, I—"

"I haven't seen him for centuries. It's his fault I'm here, chasing Temple. And because he's here again, something must have changed."

"Centuries?"

Gabriel shook his head and rowed harder.

"Gabriel, centuries?"

He said no more. Our brief conversation was over, and I had no idea when or even if it would ever begin again.

• • •

Night fell as we were on the water, and Gabriel was keen to move quickly to take advantage of the darkness. It took us a couple of hours to reach the mainland, and from there he wanted to flee the built-up areas for the jungle. I guessed that Mad Meloy's grave was maybe thirty miles inland—we'd been stopping and starting down from there, fighting, killing, dying—and Gabriel said we could make it in two days.

The way I felt right then, I was thinking two weeks.

Gabriel never let up. He was constantly on edge, talking very little but always looking as though he expected an attack at any minute. We hid from Japanese patrols, using side streets whenever we could, spending an hour here and there in abandoned gardens, and he never seemed to tire.

Now and then, I tried to question him again. "Centuries, Gabriel?" I asked. He mostly said nothing, or if he did reply, it was to tell me I would never understand. I wished he would let me be the judge of that.

We passed several areas that had been flattened by bombing and shelling, and which now were all but deserted. A few people wandered around, blasted into shock, seemingly aimless but always needing to move on. Dogs scampered through the rubble, and they looked well-fed. We never saw any Japanese patrols in these places—almost as if they had no wish to occupy the ruins—and so, we travelled through them as much as possible. It slowed our progress but made it less dangerous.

"Is he close?" I asked as we rested in a rubble-strewn garden.

Gabriel shook his head. "Not right now. I think he's still back on the island."

"Then we're away from him!"

"It doesn't work like that. He'll find out where we are, and he'll come."

"How will he find out? No one else knows."

"He has his ways and means."

I thought of Sergeant Major Snelling running from that house, the terror on his face, and then the demon thing flexing his hand as he followed. Ways and means. I had no wish to witness them myself.

Gabriel seemed able to move without being seen. He

knew the correct routes to take, sensed his way past Japanese units or gatherings of locals, steering us safely on a midnight journey through a place that should have offered us danger. The night was not without its tensions—sometimes, I was afraid to breathe lest I be overheard by the enemy—but as dawn tinged the horizon, I truly began to believe that Gabriel would see us through.

And I was growing more afraid of him with every hour that passed.

On the second day, we moved away from the built-up areas and the landscape turned more to jungle. We stopped for breakfast and I broke open a tin of processed meat. I offered some to Gabriel, but he was uninterested. I drank, and Gabriel refused the water.

"How long can you go on without eating or drinking?" I asked.

"Until I'm hungry and thirsty."

I ate more meat. As the sun rose, I realised that I knew this place. "A mile up there is where Davey bought it," I said. "Brave bastard."

"He said nothing else to you about the man in the jungle?"

"I don't think so."

"You're sure?"

"We'd just been machine-gunned and my friend was dying. I can't remember every word he said, so, no, I'm not sure. Can't you see into my head to check?" I leaned forward and tried to stare at him, but I looked quickly away. His eye was just too strange.

"No, I can't see into your head."

"Then trust me. He told me about something he'd written down, said it was important. Then mentioned the man with a snake in his eye. Whatever that means."

"Whatever, indeed." Gabriel reached for the water canteen and let a few drops speckle his tongue. He touched his forehead and sighed. "We should go. He's coming."

"How come you know when he's after you?"

"He gave me these wounds. They remember him."

Just what the hell had I got myself mixed up in there?

. . .

We followed a road into the jungle. Occasionally, the roar of a motor forced us to hide in the undergrowth, but by mostly staying to the road, we made good progress. This was the way we had come days before, shoved ahead of the Japanese force like the bow wave of a boat. We were passing places where men I knew had died, and here and there, we smelled the distinctive aroma of rot. Sometimes, the rotten things wore Japanese uniforms, but I found no particular joy in that. I had never found it in my heart to truly hate the enemy, but as time went on—and I saw more of what was happening in and around Changi and Singapore—I found less cause for forgiveness.

I had been training to be a bricklayer when war broke out. I was a good man, so I believed, as were those who had fought and died around me. None of us deserved this.

And I was feeling more and more used by Gabriel, as though I were a tool dragged behind him rather than a man. He rarely spoke to me, and when he did, it was to ask yet again what Davey had said when he was dying, how he had described the man in the jungle. I came to believe he was trying to make me slip up with my story. Did he think I was lying? Or did he simply not trust my memory?

We walked all through that day, narrowly avoiding one Japanese patrol by hiding in a culvert beneath the road. We stayed there for some time and I fell asleep, weariness overtaking my concern and giving me a few precious minutes' respite from the heat, tiredness and fear. When I woke up, Gabriel was staring at me—really staring—analysing my face and neck.

"You look so normal," he said.

"I am. I was."

"I can't remember being normal."

"Centuries, Gabriel?"

"Centuries." He did not elaborate. And it was that unwillingness to talk, more than anything else I had seen or would yet see, that made me believe.

Centuries.

Eleven

THEY CONTINUED THROUGH THE NIGHT. They moved slower than during the day, and though the heat was not as bad, there were what felt like a million mosquitoes bugging them, feeding on their sweat and the blood on Gabriel's face. He felt them tickling the inside of his hollowed eye socket. Sykes kept up well, though Gabriel suspected they would have to rest when dawn arrived.

Temple was on their trail. He had discovered their escape and now he was following, using whatever strange means he had to track them up through Malaya and into the heart of the jungle. Gabriel knew that he had to prepare to take on the demon yet again, and a collage of images kept flooding his mind's eye, visions of Temple in dozens of the fights they had been through—screaming, shouting, laughing. Always laughing. Virtually every time they met, Temple would get away, and Gabriel would be left with another scar. Nothing was ever resolved. There was no end, and a resolution to this quest felt as distant as ever.

Until now.

The man with the snake in his eye had been there, and somewhere ahead of them was a grave that could hold wonders.

"I'll need to rest soon," Sykes said, and then he started coughing as a breeze tainted the air around them. It was the smell of pained death. There was not just rotten meat there but rage, hopelessness and dead prayers. Somewhere ahead lay a scene from Hell, and something told Gabriel that it could be linked to his quest.

"We need to push on," he said. Without waiting for a reply, he left the road and plunged into the jungle. He was following his nose.

Sykes soon caught up with him, breathing hard. "We're close," he said. "I think I recognise the bend in the road back there, by the fallen tree. We're close. Maybe half a mile into the jungle, there's a small river, and that's where we fought. For a while, at least, before the bastards moved on to set up their next ambush."

"And this is where Mad Meloy is buried? Close to here?"

"Very close. But . . . I never saw his grave."

"What?"

"Davey buried him. I know roughly where. And there'll be a marker."

"If your Davey had any sense, he'd have left no sign—"

"There'll be a marker." Sykes sounded definite, and angry that Gabriel would even doubt him. "No way Davey would have left Meloy out here alone and unknown."

They went on, pushing through undergrowth, and the first body was a dead Japanese soldier. They passed him by, and Gabriel knew this was not the source of the smell. *There's more*, he thought. *More to this than death. There's . . .*

"Holy fucking shit," Sykes said.

There was a clearing in the jungle, not too dissimilar from the place back in Wales where Gabriel used to sit and muse as a normal man. Around this clearing stood trees and wild clumps of foliage, and tied to them—at ground level or higher—were dead men. Some were crucified between the trunks of two trees growing close together. Others were tied closer to the ground, a bucket of water left before them as torture. One man had been pinned to a tree, a broken branch protruding from his abdomen. All of them were emaciated—that much was obvious even in death—and those who had not died of their immediate injuries must have starved to death.

"Bastards," Sykes muttered. He walked into the clearing, seemingly ignoring the stench. "British, Australians, Indians," he said. "They didn't differentiate. Didn't care. Look."

Gabriel looked, and even he felt an element of shock. In a spread of young bamboo lay a dead man. The only reason he was still on the ground was because he had been staked there. Two dozen bamboo shoots had grown through him, distorting his body. They were dark with dried blood, and ants, flies and beetles buzzed the wounds.

"This may not have been the Japanese," Gabriel said.

"Your demon could do all this?"

"With ease."

"Why?"

And then Gabriel heard the voice he had been dreading.

"Bait," Temple said. "Hello, Gabriel."

• • •

"You didn't do this."

Temple looked around and shrugged. "How do you know?"

"Because I see your eyes," Gabriel said. "And you're fascinated."

The man who could have been a demon then looked directly at me. "So, has this one-eyed madman told you all those strange stories about me? Called me a monster? Said he and I have been fighting down through the centuries, battling here, scrapping there? Did he tell you about the pirate ship, and Queen Victoria, and the Antarctic expedition? Such an imagination."

"He told me centuries, and I believe him."

"Why? He's insane."

"I've seen you before," I said. I took a step closer to Gabriel, relying on my knowledge about Mad Meloy's grave to afford me some protection. Other than that, I sensed that I was nothing to these two beings. They existed somewhere else, a place where the war did not matter other than being a different venue for their conflict.

"Oh, you mean this?" Temple flickered, and his face became that of the Japanese officer, just for a second. Then he was back to the tall blond man. He had changed his clothes somewhere, and now he looked like a thousand other captured soldiers. All except the eyes. None of them could have those eyes.

"I have something else on my side," Gabriel said.

"You always have someone or something else on your side. You usually lose."

"Usually."

Temple walked from the shadow of a tree and through the new bamboo growth. As he stepped on the dead man's chest, a rattle sounded in the corpse's throat. "See? Even the dead think you're a joke."

Gabriel glanced sideways at Sykes. "Don't look at his

hand," he whispered.

"This?" Temple called.

"Close your eyes if you have to."

"Surely he wants to see? What scares you, Sykes?"

"Don't look," Gabriel said. "And when the time comes, go for the grave. I'll meet you there."

"And if you don't?" I asked.

"One look, that's all!" the demon called, almost cheery.

"Then he'll meet you there. And if he does, you can't let him see whatever you find. You can't!"

There was so much in Gabriel's eyes, so many things unsaid, frightening things that I think he'd been holding back. I did not know who to believe—the man who could change his face, or this man who told me he was centuries old. Both were unbelievable.

"I won't," I said.

"One glance, soldier boy, and all this death will seem like child's play." I looked, only for a second, and somehow I kept my eyes away from his hand. It was shimmering there—something was moving—but I tore my gaze away, turned and ran into the jungle.

I looked back just once, in time to see Gabriel kneel, swing his arm around and throw his knife in one fluid movement. It struck Temple in the face, and I heard the crunch of breaking bone. He fell to his knees. I slowed, then stopped.

Gabriel turned and glared at me, blood pouring from his eye. "Run!" he shouted.

Behind him, Temple stood.

I ran.

Twelve

I HEARD THE FIGHT BEGINNING. I did not hear it end. As I ran, I heard the screams, the battle cries, the snap of breaking bones and the animal grunts of unarmed combat. It faded the further I ran, and when I came across the small river where we had been ambushed, the sound of running water carried the fight away.

I made my way through the water, pausing for a quick drink. My heart was hammering. This was unreal, yet it felt so immediate. My skin tingled, my hair stood on end, and I ignored my tiredness and forged ahead.

I found the place where I had hunkered down as Meloy lobbed grenades toward the Japanese. The jungle echoed with the ghost sounds of gunfire and screams, and skeins of smoke seemed to drift between leaves, touching branches and blooms with their rank fingers. I moved a few steps, and the scene moved into the past once more; just one small shift of perspective changed everything. I listened for the sounds of Gabriel and Temple fighting, but there was nothing. Perhaps I had gone too far.

Trying to remember where Davey had emerged from the jungle after the battle, I climbed a small hill. Where bushes grew high I crawled beneath them, and where they hugged the ground I shoved ferns and branches aside, looking around for the marker I knew Davey would have left on Mad Meloy's grave. He'd been a religious man, and he would not have buried his friend and left no sign.

I was terrified, and excited, and thrilled to be away from the Japanese. Even the war felt more distant than it had for the last three years. I'd been in France, plucked from the beach at Dunkirk, trained in Southern England and then shipped out here, and in all that time, I had never felt so remote from the world as I did right then. It was as if I was on another path, a road travelled by Gabriel and his demon, parallel to our own and yet barely troubled by reality.

"Being used," I whispered. "That's me. Just being used."

Something moved behind me. I dropped to the ground and twisted around, watching a fern wave to a standstill. There was no breeze, no movement. Insects buzzed and a bird cawed somewhere above me, unconcerned at whatever might be hiding out there.

I hurried on, still climbing the shallow hill. I came across a couple of dead Japanese and walked between them, pausing to pluck a bayonet from one of their belts. I discarded the small kitchen knives I'd brought along with me, amazed that I'd thought they could help. It felt good to be carrying a proper weapon again.

In the distance, a scream.

I paused, ducked down, and through a tangle of roots and stems I saw a rough marker stuck in the ground a dozen steps away. It was the shovel that had been used to dig the grave, stuck in the ground, handle broken. "There," I said. I crawled, twisting my way through the undergrowth.

It was a shallow grave dug in the frenzy of post-battle confusion. I reached across, clawed my hand and pulled back a tangle of dried roots and mud, exposing the tip of an army boot.

"Hi, Meloy," I said. "So, what are you hiding in there?"

"Sykes!"

I screamed. I couldn't help it. I must have been so tightly wound that hearing my name hissed from the undergrowth caused me to vent my tension. The scream was short and abrupt, accompanied by the tripling of my heart rate. I rolled onto my back and scurried backward, trying to hide the grave with my body while brandishing the bayonet.

Gabriel stumbled his way through the bushes. He was bleeding and battered, rips in his clothing matching the rents in his flesh beneath. But there was something in his expression that set my skin afire. Something like victory.

Thirteen

"IT CAN'T END LIKE THIS," Gabriel said. He lay staring at the sky, the piercing blue framed by the tops of trees. Birds spotted the sky, their shadows distorted by heat. "It can't end like this."

This journey had a reason. Its culmination had meaning. It was not simply another chase to reach some unfortunate assassination victim before Temple. Gabriel had been on countless quests like that, and many of them had ended badly for him. But this had been different. Amidst so much chaos and pain and death, he had allowed himself to hope. Something had muttered to him in that garden back in Italy—the land, the voice of history, or maybe God—and he had foolishly assumed that this would finally give him an advantage over the demon.

But there was no advantage over Temple. He was a monster. As he held Gabriel down and drove the bamboo point into his stomach, he had whispered in his ear, telling Gabriel about the noises his family had made as they died, the pleas, the tears they had shed.

Gabriel's thrashing simply made the pain worse.

He raised his head and looked down at the bamboo protruding from him. Two in his stomach, one through the meat of each thigh, all of them driven into the damp ground to pin him there like an exhibit. Temple had fooled him into dropping his defences. Flashed him his hand, asked Gabriel what scared him, while all the time they both knew what would appear there.

"Bastard!" Gabriel shouted.

He would not die. He had taken a lot more than this and survived, and something had happened to him all those centuries before to ensure that he would always be there to pursue Temple. But though he would not die, neither would he live again in peace.

Peace. A strange idea. Gabriel guessed that if he did ever defeat the demon, he might have a day of peace before time finally caught up with him. It was a day he craved more than any in existence.

He reached down and grabbed one of the sticks piercing his stomach. It was slick with his sprayed blood. He tried to pull, but the pain was too much, and he knew that he would be far too late.

As Temple had entered the jungle in pursuit of Jack Sykes, Gabriel had asked him the question that had been vexing him for days: "Why did you come here?"

"Same reason as you," Temple had replied. "I was sent."

. . .

Gabriel had never seen a ghost.

He heard nothing, but he sensed the movement from the corner of his eye. He turned and looked across the surface of the ground. There was a body obscuring his view, the eyes long since taken away by rats or lizards. Beyond that, the air at the edge of the clearing shimmered as a tall shape appeared.

Gabriel closed his eyes. Was he really dying? Would he at last meet his wife and children again?

When he looked, he saw Jack Sykes standing there, dead. His eyes were wide and shocked, his throat ripped out, and his expression told that he had been driven insane before death.

"What did you see, Jack?" Gabriel asked.

The ghost walked across the clearing. At first, it seemed solid, but it passed through a dead man hanging low between two squat trees. It paused for a second, tilting its head as though it had heard screaming.

Why come back here? Gabriel thought. *Not for me. Surely not for me.*

He looked around, expecting to see Temple appear at any moment to revel in another victory. But he guessed that the demon knew nothing about this ghost. He was used to his victims going down and staying down. Fear did that to a soul.

"Can you hear?" Gabriel whispered. "Can you speak?"

The ghost ignored him. It moved across the clearing and paused before a man crucified against a tree. Gabriel could not see the spirit's face, but it seemed to be examining the corpse. Then it reached out.

"I'm here," Gabriel said.

The ghost continued to ignore him. Its hand passed into the chest of the dead man, sinking to the wrist, and then it moved its arm, head still tilted to one side.

It looked as though it was listening. And writing.

Finished, the ghost moved back across the clearing. It paused here and there to stare nowhere, its face still twisted by the madness borne by its soul at the point of its murder.

"I'm sorry, Sykes," Gabriel said. He had no idea whether or not the dead man heard. The ghost vanished back between the trees, forever lost.

• • •

It took Gabriel until sundown to remove the bamboo stakes. He was beyond exhaustion, beyond thirst and agony, and as the last stake slid out, he felt something like hope bleeding from his body.

The only thing that had prevented him from lying there, pinned to the ground and waiting to see what time would bring, was the thought of Sykes's ghost wandering into the clearing and touching the corpse.

He sat up, fighting a wave of nausea that threatened to knock him out for the night. He bit his lip and pinched the webbing between thumb and forefinger, the pain surprisingly sharp beneath the agony of the bamboo piercings.

Eventually, he managed to stand. He made his way across the clearing, sidestepping the ragged corpse of a dead soldier. Roots conspired to trip him, and fatigue almost brought him down. But the sudden vivid memory of that whisper in Italy—breeze, dust and leaves—drove him on.

He reached the body hanging on the tree and tugged at its boots until it fell.

Behind it, scored into the tree's thin bark by the fingers of a dead man, was the secret from Mad Meloy's grave. A secret that Temple now knew as well.

One word: "Armageddon."

And a date.

About the Author

TIM LEBBON is a *New York Times* bestselling writer from South Wales. He's had more than thirty novels published to date, as well as hundreds of novellas and short stories. His latest novel is the thriller *The Hunt,* and other recent releases include *The Silence* and *Alien: Out of the Shadows.* He has won four British Fantasy Awards, a Bram Stoker Award, and a Scribe Award, and has been a finalist for World Fantasy, International Horror Guild and Shirley Jackson Awards. Future books include *The Rage War* (an Alien/Predator trilogy), and the Relics trilogy from Titan.

The movie of his story *Pay the Ghost,* starring Nicolas Cage, is out now, and other projects in development include *Playtime* (an original script with Stephen Volk), *My Haunted House* with Gravy Media, *The Hunt, Exorcising Angels* (based on a novella with Simon Clark), and a TV series proposal of *The Silence.*

Find out more about Tim at his website: www.timlebbon.net.

TOR·COM

Science fiction. Fantasy. The universe.

And related subjects.

*

More than just a publisher's website, *Tor.com*

is a venue for **original fiction, comics,** and

discussion of the entire field of SF and fantasy,

in all media and from all sources. Visit our site

today—and join the conversation yourself.